THE BEARS' HOLIDAY

By Sta... ...enstain

HarperCollins Children's Books

Trademark of Random House Inc., Authorised User HarperCollins Publishers Ltd.

CONDITIONS OF SALE

This edition published in the UK by HarperCollins Children's Books in 2009

5 7 9 10 8 6 4

ISBN 13: 978-0-00-730580-3

A Beginner Book published by arrangement with Random House Inc., New York, USA
First published in Great Britain 1969

Visit our website: www.harpercollins.co.uk

Printed and bound in Hong Kong

Hooray! Hooray!
We're on our way!
Our summer holiday
starts today!

And here we are.
What a wonderful trip!
Let's get in the water!
Let's go for a dip!

Small Bear! Small Bear!
Don't you go too far.
I want to see you
wherever you are.

Don't you worry.

Don't you fear.

I'll show him

all the dangers here.

I'm watching, Dad!
I'm all set to go!

Then here is the first rule
you should know.
Obey all warning signs!
Look around.
Are there any warning signs
to be found?

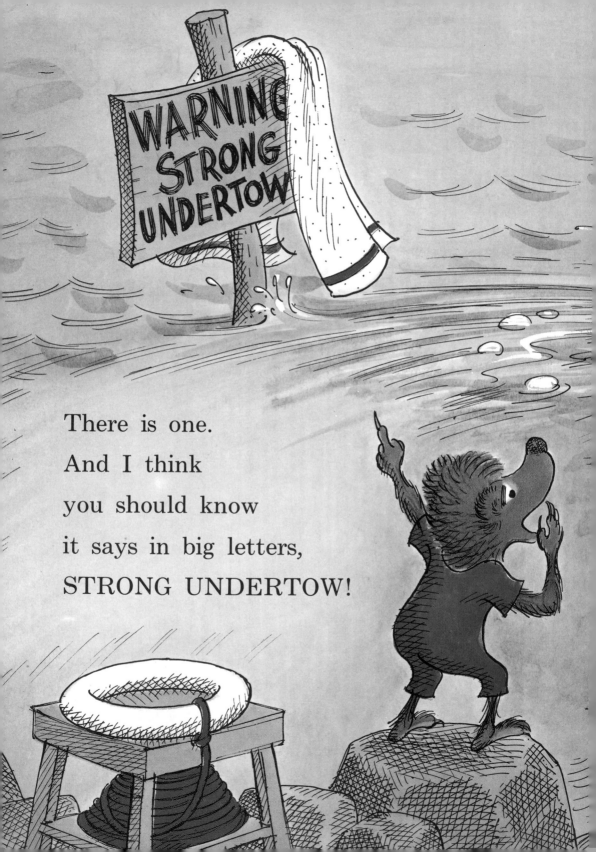

There is one.
And I think
you should know
it says in big letters,
STRONG UNDERTOW!

Ah, yes, Small Bear.
You're right! It does!
Do you see how good
my first rule was?

Yes, Papa! Here!

Catch hold of this line.

I'll be safe when I swim now.

That lesson was fine.

You will be safe
when diving, too,
after I give you
rule number two.

Look first. Then dive
when all is clear.
Now let's take a look.
Is there anything near?

Yes, Dad, there is.
I see a twig!

18

Never mind that!
It's not very big.

You proved it, Dad.
Even a twig
can be bad.

Right, my son.

That is very true.

It's a pleasure to teach

these rules to you.

Dad, I'll remember
the rules you gave.
Now let's go surfing.
Let's ride on a wave.

Now we go on
to rule number three.
Beware of all rocks
when surfing at sea.

Look, Papa! Rocks!
Right there ahead!
We should beware of them
as you said.

Those rocks are much
too far away.
The surf will not
reach those rocks today.

Then, on the other hand,
we might
end up on those rocks.
You see? I was right!

I think I understand
safety now.
Thank you, Dad,
for showing me how!

But I have much more
to tell you, my son.
My safety rules
have only begun!

When people holiday
at the shore,
they like to take walks.
They like to explore.

33

So watch your step
is rule number four.
There are many sharp shells
along the shore.

35

Here's a sharp one!
I'll step with care.
But may I keep it?
It looks quite rare.

Wait now! Don't touch
anything yet!
There's another rule
you have to get!

Here it is . . .
rule number five.
Watch what you touch.
It may be alive!

Rules four and five
are good to know.
Now I'll be safe
wherever I go.

Not quite, my son.
Hop into this boat!
You must learn the rule
for safety afloat!

Out in a boat,

you must take care.

And here is rule number six,

Small Bear.

Keep a sharp lookout!

It's easy to do.

Watch me, now!

I'll do it for you!

See? Like this!
Only a fool
would sail on the sea
without this rule!

It's a very good rule.
I can see that, Dad.
Without it, things might
get very bad!

I've been happy to learn
all you had to teach.
Are we ready, now,
to go back to the beach?

I have one rule more
before we go,
and then you'll know
all you need to know.

One more thing
people do at the shore. . .
they go underwater
and explore.

In exploring
underwater places,
there are many, many
dangerous spaces.

And my last rule
is simple and clear:
Stay out of caves
when exploring down here!

Hmmm. This cave
is big and wide!
It might be safe
to go inside.

But, Papa, do you
think you should?
Something tells me
it wouldn't be good!

As I was saying,
stay out of small spaces,
and any other
dangerous places!

WOW!
We learned that rule
very fast!

Tell me, Dad,
was that the last?

Yes, that rule
was the very last one.
My safe holiday rules
are done!

Ma!
You won't have to worry
any more!
Pa taught me how
to be safe at the shore!

Learning to read is fun with Beginner Books

I CAN READ IT ALL BY MYSELF

Beginner Books

FIRST get started with:

Ten Apples Up On Top
Dr. Seuss

Go Dog Go
P D Eastman

Put Me in the Zoo
Robert LopShire

THEN gain confidence with:

Dr. Seuss's ABC*
Dr. Seuss

Fox in Sox*
Dr. Seuss

Green Eggs and Ham*
Dr. Seuss

Hop on Pop*
Dr. Seuss

I Can Read With My Eyes Shut
Dr. Seuss

I Wish That I Had Duck Feet
Dr. Seuss

One Fish, Two Fish*
Dr. Seuss

Oh, the Thinks You Can Think!
Dr. Seuss

Please Try to Remember the First of October
Dr. Seuss

Wacky Wednesday
Dr. Seuss

Are You My Mother?
P D Eastman

Because a Little Bug Went Ka-choo!
Rosetta Stone

Best Nest
P D Eastman

Come Over to My House
Theo. LeSieg

The Digging-est Dog
Al Perkins

I Am Not Going to Get Up Today!
Theo. LeSieg

It's Not Easy Being a Bunny!
Marilyn Sadler

I Want to Be Somebody New
Robert LopShire

Maybe You Should Fly a Jet!
Theo. LeSieg

Robert the Rose Horse
Joan Heilbroner

The Very Bad Bunny
Joan Heilbroner

THEN take off with:

The Cat in the Hat*
Dr. Seuss

The Cat in the Hat Comes Back*
Dr. Seuss

Oh Say Can You Say?
Dr. Seuss

My Book About Me
Dr. Seuss

A Big Ball of String
Marion Holland

Chitty Chitty Bang Bang!
Ian Fleming

A Fish Out of Water
Helen Palmer

A Fly Went By
Mike McClintock

The King, the Mice and the Cheese
N & E Gurney

Sam and the Firefly
P D Eastman

BERENSTAIN BEAR BOOKS
By Stan & Jan Berenstain

The Bear Detectives

The Bear Scouts

The Bears' Christmas

The Bears' Holiday

The Bears' Picnic

The Berenstain Bears and the Missing Dinosaur Bones

The Big Honey Hunt

The Bike Lesson

THEN you won't quite be ready to go to college. But you'll be well on your way!

*From the Dr. Seuss Classic Collection